THE PUPPY PLACE

ZIPPER

THE PUPPY PLACE

Don't miss any of these other stories by Ellen Miles!

THE PUPPY PLACE

ZIPPER

ELLEN MILES

SCHOLASTIC INC.

For my best pal Zipper,
and for Wayne

ISBN 978-0-545-60381-2

Cover art by Tim O'Brien
Original cover design by Steve Scott

12 11 10 9 8   15 16 17 18 19/0

Printed in the U.S.A.   40

First printing, January 2014

CHAPTER ONE

"Icicle! Icicle!" Lizzie pointed out the car window. "See it? It's *huge*!"

Her best friend, Maria, pretended to yawn. "We've already seen about forty thousand icicles."

"I know," said Lizzie. "But come on, that gigantic one was special."

Maria shrugged. She did not look impressed. "I'll give you half a point."

"Fine," said Lizzie. "But then you only get half a point for that leftover Christmas wreath. We've seen a billion of them, too."

The girls were in the backseat of the Santiagos' car, heading north. Maria's parents had invited

Lizzie along on their annual winter-break trip to Bear Valley, a ski area in Maine. The trip was long, much longer than the ride to the Santiagos' cabin, where Lizzie had spent some time. Lizzie and Maria had already played Twenty Questions and I Spy. Now they were playing Winter Bingo, spotting special things they could see only because it was cold and snowy. They got a point for each item they claimed — but since they were making the rules up as they went along, the girls were doing more arguing than spotting.

Lizzie was used to arguing with her two brothers, but Charles and the Bean usually gave in to her at some point, since she was the oldest. Maria was tougher. Lizzie had to admire the way her friend held her ground.

"Snowman! Snow-woman! A whole snow family!"

Maria jumped up and down in her seat as she pointed. "That's worth two points."

"Two points? Are you crazy?" Lizzie glared at her friend.

"Girls." Mr. Santiago spoke up from the driver's seat. "How about if we all just sit back and enjoy the scenery quietly for a little while? We're just coming into the prettiest, wildest part of the drive."

"I second that," said Mrs. Santiago. She sat in the passenger seat up front, knitting. Mrs. Santiago was an amazing knitter. She was blind, so she did it all by touch. Sometimes Maria helped her sort her yarn, but then she'd be on her way, creating soft, thick rainbows of color. She'd made Maria a gorgeous pair of mittens and a matching scarf for Christmas, all in shades of blue and green.

Simba woofed softly from the way-back seat.

Mrs. Santiago laughed. "He's voting for quiet, too." Of course she could translate Simba's woofs. Simba, a solid, dignified yellow Lab, was Mrs. Santiago's guide dog.

Lizzie reached back to give Simba a scratch between the ears. "Well, if Simba says so . . ." In Lizzie's opinion, dogs ruled. She was crazy about dogs of every breed. Lizzie loved to train dogs, play with dogs, learn about dogs, draw dogs, and dream about the dogs she might have in the future. She and Maria even had a dog-walking business. Fortunately, they shared it with two friends, who were taking care of things while Maria and Lizzie were away.

Petting Simba made Lizzie miss Buddy, her puppy. She knew she was lucky to be going on this vacation, but a little part of her wished she were home with Buddy, curled up together on her bed or playing in the backyard. Lizzie's fingers itched to pet the heart-shaped white spot in the middle of his soft brown chest.

The Petersons fostered puppies, taking care of each one until they found it the perfect forever home. If it were up to Lizzie, her family would keep every single puppy they fostered, but that was never going to happen. At least she'd gotten to keep Buddy.

"Miss him?" Maria looked sympathetic.

Lizzie raised her eyebrows. Had Maria read her mind?

"You're thinking about Buddy, right?" Maria asked. "I can always tell. You get this certain look on your face. Don't worry. Soon you're going to be having so much fun at Bear Valley that you won't miss him at all." She pulled a map out of the seat-back pocket in front of her. "See, our lodge is right here." She pointed. "At the base of Little Bear

Mountain. Little Bear's my favorite, the one with all the best trails. The terrain park is there, too. You know, with all the jumps and stuff. You won't believe how cool it is."

Lizzie peered at the map, trying to make sense of the tangle of trails. This whole ski-resort thing was new to her. She had tried cross-country skiing one time, in Vermont, but she had not been very good at it. She'd tried snowshoeing, too, and she had liked that better. She'd even had the chance to drive a dogsled! What an adventure that had been. She smiled, thinking of the gorgeous husky pup named Bear that her family had ended up fostering on that trip.

"You're going to love this trail." Maria pointed. "Grizzly. It's a little steep, but so much fun!"

"Woo-hoo!" said Mrs. Santiago. "Grizzly's one of my favorites, too."

Lizzie still could not imagine how Mrs. Santiago could be brave enough to ski without being able to see, but Maria had told her how much her mother loved to whiz down the slopes in her bright orange vest, with another skier whizzing along next to her, making sure she didn't hit any obstacles. That was called adaptive skiing, Lizzie now knew.

Lizzie wasn't sure she'd be brave enough for a trail like Grizzly, even though she could see perfectly well. She and Maria would be snowboarding. "I can teach you in, like, ten minutes," her friend had promised. "You'll love it." Lizzie wasn't so sure about that, but she was willing to try if it meant going on vacation with her best friend.

Now Mr. Santiago's eyes met Lizzie's in the rearview mirror. He smiled. "Or you can always come hiking with me," he said. Mr. Santiago was not a skier or a snowboarder. He loved to poke through the wintry woods on snowshoes, looking for animal tracks. "This new snow should be perfect for tracking."

Lizzie looked out the window at the snowbanks that lined both sides of the small two-lane highway. Tall trees loomed above the road, their bare branches lit golden by the late-afternoon sun. There hadn't been a house or a store or any kind of building for a long time, not since the farm they'd passed with the snow family in front of its red barn. They were really in the country now.

The road twisted and turned as it climbed up, up, up into the mountains. Lizzie began to wish she had not looked at that Bear Valley map. She'd forgotten that reading in cars always made her tummy feel a little whoopsy. Now, as she sat in the backseat and they swooped through turn after turn, her tummy felt a *lot* whoopsy. She closed her eyes. That didn't help at all. She opened them and stared at the seat in front of her. *Ugh.* Not good. She looked out the window at the snow-covered trees flying by. "Ohh," she groaned. "Um, Mr. S., do you think you could —" She clutched her belly.

"Are you okay?" Maria asked. She reached out to pat Lizzie's shoulder. "You look sort of green."

Mr. Santiago glanced into the rearview mirror. "Lizzie, are you going to —" Something he saw in Lizzie's face must have answered his question. He put on his turn signal. The car slowed, pulled to the right, then skidded to a sudden stop at a strange angle. Lizzie's shoulder banged against the window, and Maria bumped up against her.

"Uh-oh," said Mrs. Santiago. "That doesn't feel right."

Mr. Santiago sighed. "No kidding. I think we just went into a ditch."

Lizzie sat up. "Can I still get out?" she asked.

"If your door will open, sure," said Mr. Santiago.

Lizzie managed to open her door just a few inches before it wedged itself against the snowbank. Still, she was able to squeeze through the small opening. When she stepped out, she sank into the snow. "Whoa," she said. "It's over my knees!"

"Careful," said Mrs. Santiago. "How do you feel?"

Lizzie took a few deep breaths of clean, cold air. "I feel fine," she said, surprised. She turned to look back at the car. "But I think we might be stuck."

Mr. Santiago got out of the car and walked around to look at the passenger-side wheels, which were both half-buried in snow. "I think you're right," he said.

Lizzie felt awful. "I'm sorry," she said in a tiny voice.

"It's not your fault." Mr. Santiago bent to scrape snow away from the front tire. "But I'm not sure how we're going to get out of here. There's no cell phone service until we get higher up in the mountains, so I can't call for a tow." He stood up and scratched his head.

"We could flag down the next car that comes along," said Maria, who had also climbed out of the car.

"Good idea," said Mr. Santiago. "But we haven't seen another car in a while. It's awfully quiet out here."

It *was* quiet, Lizzie realized. Very quiet. No wind, no traffic noises, no airplanes overhead. She held her breath for a moment, listening. Then she heard a familiar sound. She would know that sound anywhere! It was the sound of jingling collar tags. She turned to look into the woods and saw something moving toward them, leaping through the snow like a deer.

But it wasn't a deer. It was a puppy.

CHAPTER TWO

Lizzie stared. What was a puppy doing way out here, in the middle of nowhere?

"Is that a dog?" Mr. Santiago squinted.

"It sure is," said Lizzie. "And he's running right toward us — and right toward the road. Let's catch him!" She dug into her jacket pocket. She always carried dog treats: you just never knew. "Yes," she whispered as she pulled out a few pieces of freeze-dried liver, one of Buddy's favorites.

"He's *fast*!" said Maria. "I'll try to grab him if he comes this way." She moved over to a spot behind the car.

"Hey, pup! Here, pup!" Lizzie called. She held out the treat.

Amazingly, the dog charged straight toward her. He was tall and rangy, with long, muscular legs that helped him leap through the deep snow. His short coat was brown and tan, and he had silly long ears and a happy, grinning face with tan eyebrow spots. He wore a regular collar but also a red harness that wrapped around his body. A matching red lead trailed from where it was hooked at the back of the harness, near his long, thin tail.

That tail was wagging hard as the dog came right up to Lizzie. Even though she could see that he was a friendly goof, and probably very young, she thought it might not be a good idea to hand him a treat until she knew him better. She tossed a cube of dried liver onto the snow near her feet, and while he gobbled it, she reached for his collar.

"Got him!" she said just as he wriggled away from her. "Oops."

Maria popped up from behind the car. She knelt down and held her arms wide. "Come see me, pup," she called in a happy, high voice.

Curious, the dog went to check out the new person. He stretched his neck to sniff Maria's hand. "Good boy," she said softly. "Good boy." Her other hand moved around to take his collar. She stood up. "Okay, now we've really got him."

"Nice work," said Mr. Santiago. "But — now what?" He waved a hand at the car. "It was bad enough that we were stuck. Now we're stuck and we have an extra dog on our hands."

Lizzie plunged through the snow toward Maria to pet the new arrival. She had no idea what kind of dog he was, which was unusual. Normally, Lizzie could tell the breed of any dog instantly. But that harness did look familiar. "I think he might be a sled dog. Is there a snowmobile trail near here?" She remembered the sled dogs she had met in Vermont. They wore harnesses exactly like this one, and they loved to run on the wide snowmobile trails that crisscrossed the state.

Mr. Santiago peered toward the woods. "Maybe," he said doubtfully. "I know there's one near Bear Valley."

By then Mrs. Santiago had put her knitting away and climbed out of the car. "What's going on?" she asked. "Simba is all upset."

Maria explained about the dog.

"A dog? Out here?" Mrs. Santiago asked. "Does he have tags on his collar?"

Lizzie couldn't believe she had not thought of that yet. She knelt down to take a look, and the dog licked her cheek and put one of his big, chunky paws on her arm.

Hey there, hey there! Nice to meet you!

Lizzie laughed and ducked her head. "There's a rabies tag," she reported. "But nothing with a name or phone number."

"Hey! What do you think you're doing?"

They all turned at the sound of a deep voice. A tall, slim man with red cheeks skied up to them, towed by another long-legged dog, this one black with a white chest. The dog's blue eyes flashed and his tongue hung out as he pulled the cross-country skier over the snow.

"We're just —" began Mr. Santiago, but the skier was glaring at the gangly brown-and-tan puppy.

"Whoa," the skier said. The man wore a belt that was attached by a long lead to a harness on the black-and-white dog. The pair slowed to a stop. "You are in big trouble, pal." The man shook a finger at the brown-and-tan pup as he stuck his ski poles into the snow and knelt to take off his skis.

Lizzie stood up. "He came right to us," she said.

"I bet he did," said the man. "Zipper loves to meet new people." He shook his head at the dog Maria held. "You little pest."

"Zipper!" Lizzie said. "What a perfect name for this zippy guy."

The puppy hung his head and looked up at the man from the corners of his eyes.

Oops. Sorry. I was just curious.

The man sighed and smiled as he picked up the red lead hanging from Zipper's harness. He held it up to show them how it was frayed at one end.

"I'm glad he's safe, anyway. He must have chewed halfway through this while we were taking a break. Then, when he heard you, he gave one big pull and it snapped. This guy always has to know what's going on. He's a real Nosey Parker — that's what we call a busybody in these parts."

"You're a skijorer, aren't you?" Lizzie asked. She'd heard about that sport, in which one or two dogs towed a skier along a trail. She'd always thought it sounded fun — and kind of terrifying, too. You'd have to be a pretty good skier.

The man nodded. "That's right. I was skiing on the trail right over there." He waved a hand toward the trees. "I'm trying to train this pup. He's only eight months old, but he's plenty strong. He sure does love to run, but I'm afraid his curiosity is working against us. He's got to check everything out." He reached down to ruffle Zipper's ears. "Thanks for catching him."

For the first time, he looked around and seemed to realize why they were all standing outside their car. "Uh-oh," he said. "Looks like somebody could use some help."

CHAPTER THREE

The man stuck out his hand to Mr. Santiago. "I'm Dillon," he said. "You already met Zipper, and this other dog is Digger, Zipper's father."

Mr. Santiago smiled. "I'm Victor. I'm Maria's father." He put a hand on Maria's shoulder. "And that's her friend Lizzie, and my wife, Gloria, over there. Her dog, Simba, is the one fogging up the back windows." He waved to the car.

Dillon grinned around at all of them. He rubbed his hands up and down his arms. "Getting chilly out here," he said. "We'd better get you folks on your way."

Lizzie thought he must be freezing in his black tights and lightweight jacket. He was dressed for moving, not for standing still. As the sun sank behind the trees, Lizzie was beginning to feel the chill, even through the puffy down jacket she'd grabbed out of the car.

"Right," said Mr. Santiago. "Do you think we could get unstuck if you gave us a push?"

"Oh, sure," said Dillon. "No problem." He grinned again and flexed his arms. "Ask anyone: strongest man in the town of Tilden, Maine!"

Lizzie and Maria giggled.

"Are we in Tilden already?" asked Mrs. Santiago. "That's good news. I can't wait to settle into our lodge."

"Staying at the Timberline?" asked Dillon.

"How did you guess?" she asked.

"My aunt and uncle own the place," Dillon said.

"The Muellers. They love to host families with dogs."

"Exactly!" said Mrs. Santiago. "Annie and Josef. We've stayed with them many times. They're crazy about Simba."

Dillon laughed. "That sounds like them." He turned to Lizzie and Maria. "Think you two can hold the pups while we get this car out?"

Lizzie nodded. "We're professionals," she said. "Dog walkers. You can trust us."

He raised his eyebrows. "Glad to hear it." He handed her Zipper's lead. He gave Digger's to Maria. "Might be safest to walk up ahead just a bit, keep them out of the way."

Mrs. Santiago and the girls took the dogs up the road to watch. Digger was calm, but Zipper tugged at his lead, and Lizzie had to hold on with all her strength. He sniffed the ground as he raced forward. Then he stopped suddenly to paw at a snowbank. Then he turned back toward the car to see what Dillon and Mr. Santiago were doing.

What's going on? What's going on?

Lizzie laughed as Zipper tugged her this way and that. She was used to walking all sorts of dogs, and she knew how to hold tight and keep her balance. Zipper was as strong as a German shepherd, even though he was as skinny as a greyhound and had a head that looked like a dachshund's. Digger, his father, not only had completely different coloring but was built differently, too. He was bulkier, with a big blocky head. What kind of dogs *were* they? "I can see why Dillon calls you Nosey Parker," she said.

Mr. Santiago got into the car and started it up. Dillon set himself at the back bumper and called out directions. "Turn the wheels to the left," he shouted. "Good. Now give it a little gas and let it rock forward and back while I push."

The car's tires spun, creating a high-pitched whine that made Zipper's ears stand up. Lizzie noticed how he stood at attention, watching with interest as snow and ice chunks flew and the car rocked. Dillon grunted loudly as he shoved the car from behind. "Go, go, go!" he yelled. "Rev it up now!"

With one last, loud whine, the car shot up out of the ditch and back onto the road.

"Yes!" Dillon threw his fists into the air. Mr. Santiago grinned from the driver's seat as he guided the car slowly forward, then stopped with all four wheels on dry road. He hopped out to shake hands with Dillon.

"Nicely done," he said. "I can tell you've had some experience."

Dillon shrugged. "Happens all the time when you live in a snowy place. Just part of the deal." He walked over to get Digger's lead from Maria. "Thanks," he said. "We'll just barely have time to get home before dark, which is a good thing, since I forgot my headlamp."

"Would you like a ride?" asked Mr. Santiago.

"No, thanks." Dillon shook his head. "I'm training for a big race and I need all the conditioning I can get. People think the dog does all the work when you're skijoring, but I can tell you that the human gets a workout, too." He paused, looking at Zipper. "But maybe there's another favor you can do for me."

Lizzie couldn't help smiling. She had a feeling she knew what was coming.

"I don't have a spare lead with me, and he's ruined that one. Do you think you could take Zipper with you? My aunt and uncle won't mind a

bit, and I'll come collect him as soon as I've show-
ered and changed." Dillon glanced from Mr.
Santiago to Mrs. Santiago.

Lizzie was the first to answer him. "Yes! We'd
love to," she said.

CHAPTER FOUR

Maria stared at Lizzie. "Who put you in charge?" she asked.

"It's fine, Maria," said Mrs. Santiago. "Dillon, we'd love to help. We owe you for pushing us out of that ditch!"

"You don't owe me a thing, but thanks." Dillon hooked Digger's lead back to his belt, then stepped into his ski bindings. "I can tell that you're nice people. Professional dog walkers, too! I know Zipper will be safe with you. See you soon." He put his hand through the wrist loops on his poles, then told Digger to "hike!" and they were off, dashing across the snow.

Zipper watched them go, his ears alert. He stood up and began to whine as Dillon and Digger disappeared behind a line of trees.

Hey, why do they get to —

"That's enough," Lizzie told him. "You only have yourself to blame." She gave a gentle tug on his collar, turning him toward the car. "Hop in, now."

Soon they were headed down the highway again. Lizzie had helped Zipper out of his harness so he would be more comfortable, and now he sat between her and Maria, sniffing each of them in turn and then turning to exchange sniffs with a curious Simba.

Maria sighed and leaned against her window. "I should've known."

"What?" asked Lizzie.

"You just can't go anywhere without finding a dog to foster." Maria rolled her eyes. "I thought we were on vacation. We walk dogs five days a week at home. Can't we take a break?"

Lizzie had to admit that Maria was right. She did seem to find foster puppies wherever she went. But honestly, Lizzie hardly ever felt the need for a break from anything having to do with dogs. "We're not exactly fostering him," she said, putting an arm around Zipper's skinny frame and pulling him close for a kiss. His coat was short and sleek, like a Weimaraner's, but also dense, like a Lab's. His floppy ears were like a hound's, soft and silky. She still could not put her finger on what breed he might be. "We're just watching him for a couple of hours."

"That's right," said Mr. Santiago from the front seat. "And it's the least we can do for Dillon. He really helped us out of a jam."

Soon the road began to climb steeply uphill, and the snowbanks on either side grew higher. "We're almost there," said Maria. "See? You can see the lights where they have night skiing on Papa Bear Mountain."

Lizzie remembered the Bear Valley map. Papa Bear was the biggest, steepest peak, with the hardest trails. Then there were Mama Bear and Little Bear. She was glad their lodge was near Little Bear. It seemed like the friendliest mountain.

"There's the base lodge!" Maria pointed. "And the quad!"

Lizzie saw a big building with lots of windows shining yellow in the night and, above it, a chairlift that could carry four people on each seat. The lift was running, and she could see skiers and snowboarders flying down the hill under the bright lights that lit the slopes.

She barely had time to get nervous — how in the world would she get on and off that chairlift? — before Mr. Santiago pulled into a circular driveway in front of a long two-story building that looked like an oversized log cabin. "Here we are," he said.

Lizzie liked the Timberline Lodge right away. The lounge they walked into was a cozy, welcoming place with overstuffed furniture, a big stone fireplace, shelves full of books and games, and a Ping-Pong table. A pair of old wooden skis made an archway into the high-ceilinged dining room, which was filled with long picnic-style tables. Huge windows looked out onto the ski trails.

Seconds after Mr. Santiago had tapped the bell at the reception desk, a small dark-haired woman bustled out of the office. "Ah, you're here," she said. She rushed over to give hugs to all the Santiagos, including Simba. "And this must

be Lizzie. Welcome! I'm Annie. And you have" —
she peered over her half-glasses at the puppy
whose leash Lizzie held — "Zipper with you." She
knelt right down to give Zipper a hug and a kiss.
"What are you doing here, you silly boy?" She
laughed as he licked her face.

Mrs. Santiago explained while Mr. Santiago
filled out some forms at the desk. "Well, he's very
welcome," said Annie. "Zipper is my favorite
puppy ever — except for Sofie, of course." She
looked fondly down at the long-eared basset mix
who had just padded out of the office to see what
all the fuss was about. Sofie had the same brown-
and-tan coloring as Zipper, but she was as
short and wide as he was tall and thin. "I'll call
Dillon and invite him to join us for dinner."

"Annie loves animals," Maria said to Lizzie. "In
case you couldn't tell."

"Ah! My favorite family." A man with gray hair and a neatly trimmed beard emerged from the dining room, wiping his hands on a dish towel. He wore a long white apron.

"That's Josef," Maria told Lizzie.

He hugged all the Santiagos and bowed to Lizzie when they introduced her.

"Favorite family?" Mrs. Santiago asked. "I bet you say that to all your guests."

"Maybe so, maybe so," admitted Josef. "But do I make my famous meat loaf for anyone else?"

"Yum," said Maria. "And mashed potatoes?"

"And mashed potatoes," said Josef. His eye lit on Zipper. "And what is this charming young man doing here?" he asked as he bent over to scratch the puppy's head.

Zipper looked up at Josef and crinkled his mouth in a funny, toothy grin.

I know you. You've given me some tasty treats.

As soon as Dillon arrived, they all sat down to eat. After greeting Dillon happily, Zipper settled under the table between him and Lizzie. Dinner was jolly, with big platters and bowls of food passed up and down one of the long tables. "I'm so pleased you could come a couple of days early," Josef said. He told them that the lodge would fill up to the brim once the weekend started. "Thankfully, we have plenty of snow for everyone to enjoy. And more to come, according to the weatherman."

Lizzie glanced out the window at the rope tow at the bottom of Little Bear mountain, where Maria had said they would start the next morning. She'd promised that it would pull them to the top of the easiest possible slope, and that

Lizzie would be snowboarding like a pro in no time. Lizzie was not so sure.

"All this snow should be good for your big race, Dillon," said Annie. "Isn't it this weekend?"

Dillon nodded. He had hardly spoken at all during dinner, maybe because he was too busy eating. Lizzie could not believe the huge mound of mashed potatoes he had demolished. Now he shoved back his chair. "As a matter of fact, I wanted to talk to you all about that. I need to start training seriously with Digger. I'm realizing that I just don't have time to deal with Zipper as well, at least until after the race. In fact, I'm not sure he's really cut out for skijoring at all."

He leaned down to scratch Zipper's head. "He's a sweet guy, and I like him a lot, but I may have to think about finding him another home permanently. I'm pretty busy with my racing dogs, and I don't really have time to take care of an extra pet."

Lizzie sat up straighter. A real foster puppy! How much fun would it be to find the perfect home for this sweet boy?

"Anyway," Dillon went on, "for the next few days, I could really use some help. I was wondering if there was any chance at all that —"

Lizzie jumped up to interrupt him. "Yes!"

CHAPTER FIVE

Maria whirled around. "Lizzie!" she said. "You did it again."

"Oops." Lizzie put a hand over her mouth. "I mean, I'd love to help out with Zipper, if it's okay with Mr. and Mrs. Santiago and the Muellers." She reached down to pet Zipper, who lay quietly near her feet. She was already in love with this curious, active pup. Plus, maybe she would be so busy taking care of him that she wouldn't have to snowboard after all.

Mr. Santiago frowned. "Are you sure, Lizzie? It's a big responsibility, and as Maria said, you two are on vacation. You're supposed to be enjoying yourselves."

"I always enjoy myself when I'm around a dog," said Lizzie.

"And really, it's no problem to have him here," Annie put in. "Josef and I will help when we can. We'll manage, I'm sure."

It was settled. Zipper would stay with Lizzie and the others, at the Timberline Lodge. Dillon gave Lizzie a long leash with a stretchy bungee section. "He's pretty strong when he's pulling, and he doesn't really know how to walk nicely on a leash yet," he said. "So be careful, and do your best to keep him under control. You can try walking him on his harness, if that seems easier. I'll show you how to put it back on."

Lizzie nodded. She had walked dogs who liked to pull before.

"I'll bring by some of his food tomorrow," Dillon

said. "For tonight, maybe Sofie will share some of hers." He stood up and yawned. "Thanks for dinner, Uncle Josef and Aunt Annie. Love that meat loaf. I hate to eat and run, but I'm in training and I need my sleep."

"I just have to ask one thing before you go," Lizzie said. She couldn't wait a moment longer to find out the answer to the question that had been bothering her since this long-legged puppy had bounded through the snow. "What kind of dog is Zipper, anyway?"

Dillon laughed. "Everybody asks that. He and Digger are both a mix known as a Eurohound."

"A what?" Lizzie asked. She'd never heard of such a dog before.

"The mix originated in Europe, but a lot of American mushers are using them now," Dillon said, "especially for shorter, faster sprint races. He's part Alaskan husky —"

"I know about them!" interrupted Lizzie. "I fostered one, named Bear. They're not as fluffy as Siberian huskies. And they're long-legged, like Zipper."

"That's right," said Dillon. "Some Alaskans do have some Siberian in them, but it's mixed with a lot of other breeds. Anyway, a Eurohound is also part German shorthaired pointer. Mushers have found that breeding in the pointers helps make the dogs a little easier to train, since pointers want to please their masters."

"So basically, he's a mutt," said Mrs. Santiago, reaching down to run her hands over Zipper's sleek coat.

"Exactly," said Dillon. "The fastest, strongest mutt in the world."

"Wow," said Lizzie. It was not often that she learned something new about dogs, but she had never heard of Eurohounds before. She could hardly wait to call home and tell Charles all about Zipper.

After Dillon left, Lizzie and Maria took Zipper for a walk. The Little Bear ski area was quiet, dark, and empty. "Come on," said Maria. "We can take a closer look at the trail we're going on tomorrow."

Lizzie thought of pretending that Zipper was dragging her the opposite way, but she could tell that her friend really wanted her to see the trail. "Okay," she said. "Come on, Mr. Zippy." Zipper happily turned around and pranced off in the new direction. He held his tail high and wagged it back and forth.

Wherever you go, I want to go.

"See?" Maria said in a few minutes.
"See what?" Lizzie asked.

"This is it. The trail. We're on it." Maria smiled. "You couldn't even tell we were walking uphill, could you? It's practically flat." She led Lizzie to the bottom of the rope tow and explained how it worked, showing her how to grab on to the hook that the attendant would hand her. "It's a breeze," she said.

Lizzie felt the knot in her stomach loosen a little. "It looks pretty easy," she admitted. But she thought, *I'll try it once, just to make Maria happy. Then I'll say that I have to take care of Zipper.*

Back in the lodge, the girls settled in for a long game of Dog-opoly. Lizzie and Maria lay stomach-down on the rug by the fireplace, with Zipper between them. He sighed once in a while in his sleep, and Lizzie's heart melted. Zipper looked almost like a grown dog, but he was still just a baby. He lay curled in a tight ball with his long legs tucked up under his chin and his tail tickling his nose.

"Look, he has a white patch on his chest, just like Buddy does," said Maria, reaching out to pet it. "Soft, too."

Zipper's white patch wasn't in the shape of a heart, but it did have interesting black spots. His big paws were heavy and soft, and Lizzie loved the tiny golden hairs she saw glinting amid the brown. Zipper was not a pudgy, cuddly puppy like some Lizzie had known, but there was something so lovable about him. Maybe it was his goofy face and expressive ears, or the way he was always wagging his tail and looking hopeful. Whatever it was, Lizzie was under his spell.

Annie came into the room with a plate of warm chocolate-chip cookies and two glasses of milk. "Josef thought you girls might be ready for a snack," she said, putting the plate down on a table out of Zipper's reach. "We're headed off to bed. Would you like Zipper to sleep with you in your room?"

Lizzie looked at Maria. Was her friend still mad about the way Zipper had crashed their vacation? Would she want him in their room?

"Of course," said Maria. She smiled at Lizzie, and Lizzie knew: Maria was under Zipper's spell, too.

CHAPTER SIX

Lizzie woke the next morning with Zipper nestled beside her — underneath the heavy, colorful quilt that covered her bed. "You funny thing," she said to him. "What kind of dog sleeps under the covers?"

Zipper rolled onto his back and stretched out his long, muscular legs. Then he yawned, opening his mouth so wide that Lizzie could practically count his shiny white teeth. His yawn made a noise like a creaky gate swinging open.

Mmmm, so cozy. Hey! What's that I smell?

Zipper leapt out of bed before Lizzie could pet him. He went straight to the door of Lizzie and Maria's room and sniffed along the crack at the bottom. Now Lizzie smelled it, too. "Yum," she said. "Bacon."

Maria sat up in her bed on the other side of the room and rubbed her eyes. "G'morning," she said. "How's Zipper?"

"He slept really well," Lizzie reported. "But now that he smells that bacon, he's ready to get his day going."

"So am I," said Maria. "Josef makes the best breakfasts. Wait till you taste his popovers with strawberry jam." She pulled on her long underwear and snow pants. "I'm glad we're up early. It's great to hit the trails before they get crowded."

Lizzie was in no hurry to "hit the trails," but she knew Zipper was probably ready for a walk. She dressed quickly, then helped him into his harness. He knew just how to lift one foot, then the other so she could pull it over his head. "I'll take Zipper out and meet you in the dining room," she told Maria.

Lizzie headed down the hall and slipped out the back door of the lodge. Zipper pulled hard, dragging her down the wooden stairs and onto the snow. He was following the same path they'd taken the night before. "Uh-uh," Lizzie said, guiding him away from the ski trails. The lifts were not running yet, but skiers were already lining up.

Zipper sniffed eagerly, checking everything out. Lizzie noticed the muscles working in his legs; this dog was a real athlete. She could imagine him running for miles and miles. "Not today, though, Zip," she told him as they went back inside. Poor Zipper. He probably didn't want to be cooped up in the lodge any more than she wanted to go snowboarding.

After she had fed Zipper his breakfast, Lizzie sat down with the Santiagos at one of the dining room tables. Josef hovered around them, offering scrambled eggs, bacon, and pancakes from large platters. A basket heaped with muffins, popovers, and bagels sat in the middle of the table. Next to that Lizzie saw a crock of butter, jars of honey and homemade jam, and a pitcher of maple syrup. "Wow," she said.

"I know, isn't it awesome?" Maria piled her plate high. "Eat up. You'll need your energy for shredding gnar."

Lizzie rolled her eyes. Maria loved to show off her snowboarding words. "I'll be happy if I can stay in one piece." Quietly, she hid a small piece of bacon inside her napkin. She knew better than to feed Zipper from the table; she'd give it to him later. "No gnar necessary."

After breakfast, Lizzie gave Zipper his treat. She hated to leave him. He was so sweet, especially when he looked at her with those shiny brown eyes and gave her one of his big, chunky paws to shake.

Thanks for that amazing treat. Is there any more?

Lizzie was so full of breakfast that she almost wished she could go right back to bed for a nice, cozy nap with Zipper. But Mr. Santiago scratched Zipper's ears. "Go ahead, girls," he said. "I'll keep an eye on Zipper and take him out if he needs a walk."

Lizzie and Maria helped Mrs. Santiago take her ski things to the bottom of the quad, where she had agreed to meet her adaptive-skiing partner. Then Lizzie scooped up the snowboard she'd borrowed from Maria's cousin, and followed her friend to the rope tow. Lizzie glanced back at the Timberline Lodge and saw Mr. Santiago waving from the window. Zipper was next to him, his front feet up on the windowsill as he watched the action. Lizzie giggled and waved back. "See you later, Nosey Parker," she called.

The rope tow wasn't bad. Lizzie got the hang of it right away. She liked the feeling of sliding uphill. It was sliding *downhill* that she wasn't so sure about. But when they got off the lift, Maria showed her how to stand on her snowboard and how to balance. Before she knew it, Lizzie was sailing down the slight incline. She shifted her weight and the board turned, just as Maria had said it would. Finally, she came to a stop near the bottom of the trail. She turned to Maria. "That was a blast!" she said. "Let's do it again!"

"I told you," said Maria. "You're a natural."

They scooted over to the rope tow again and took another ride up, and another. After their third trip down, Maria gave Lizzie a high five. "You're ready for the chairlift," she said. "Let's go hit some real hills."

Lizzie hesitated. "One more run on this one," she said.

"Whatever you want," said Maria. They took the rope tow up again. This time on the way down, Lizzie felt so confident that she started to experiment with quicker turns. "Whee!" she shouted as she picked up a little speed. "I'm really flying now!" Then, out of the corner of her eye, she saw something coming toward her: a blur of brown and tan. "No! Zipper, stop!" Lizzie shouted just as the leggy puppy leapt into her path. Down she went, falling hard onto the packed snow.

Zipper jumped on top of her, licking her face and snorting happily.

I thought I heard you! I knew I could find you!

Lizzie sat up and pushed him away. A bolt of pain shot through her wrist. "Oh!" she cried. "My arm!"

CHAPTER SEVEN

Everything seemed to happen at once. Maria tackled Zipper, diving on top of him to hold him down until she could grab the leash that trailed behind him. Mr. Santiago ran up, panting and apologizing. Lizzie sat on the snow and rocked back and forth, holding her arm. The guy who ran the rope tow shut it down, then dashed over to help Lizzie take off her snowboard. He talked into a radio as he worked on her bindings. "Lift One to ski patrol base. Do you copy?"

"Ow. Ow, ow, ow." Lizzie hated to sound like a baby, but she couldn't help it. Her wrist really hurt.

Zipper squirmed in Maria's grasp and poked his nose into Lizzie's face, snuffling at her ear.

What happened? Did I hurt you? Are you okay?

Lizzie couldn't help petting his head with her good hand. "It's all right," she told him. Zipper had not hurt her on purpose. He was just being his Nosey Parker self, running over to see her.

"We were out for a walk, and then he must have heard you. He pulled so hard I couldn't hang on," said Mr. Santiago. He squatted down next to Lizzie. "Are you okay?"

"Um," said Lizzie. "I don't think so." Her arm hurt so bad that it was making her stomach feel almost as whoopsy as it had in the car the day before.

"Well, we'll soon find out," said a woman in a red jacket, who had just skied down to them.

She clicked out of her skis and stuck them into the snow behind Lizzie. "I'm Sarah," she said. "I'm with the ski patrol here. What's your name?"

Sarah was so friendly and so nice that Lizzie felt better right away. She told Sarah her name and age. Mr. Santiago explained that he was responsible for Lizzie, and together they went over what had happened. Sarah gently felt Lizzie's wrist and asked her whether anything else hurt. "We can take a better look at this in our patrol room clinic," she said. "It's not far from here, but I'm going to call for a toboggan and we'll give you a ride. How does that sound?"

"Okay," said Lizzie. All she wanted was for her wrist to stop hurting.

Sarah stepped away to speak into her radio. When she came back, she shook a finger at Zipper. "You little troublemaker," she said. "Don't you know dogs don't belong on the slopes?" She scratched his ears and he grinned at her.

I didn't mean any harm. I was just checking things out.

"Isn't this one of Dillon Goss's dogs? He sure is a cutie," said Sarah. "But we'd better get him out of here before he causes another accident."

"It's Zipper," said Lizzie. "We're sort of fostering him."

"I'll take him back to our lodge." Maria patted Lizzie's shoulder. "Sorry," she said. "You were doing so well, too."

"It's not your fault," Lizzie said. "You were a good teacher. I was really getting it, wasn't I?"

"You were awesome," said Maria.

"Here's our ride," said Sarah as another ski patroller skied into view, towing a toboggan behind him. "This is Butch. He's a great driver, so you have nothing to worry about."

Butch and Sarah put Lizzie's wrist into a sling so it wouldn't move around. "I'm going to sit behind you in the sled," Sarah told her. "You can lean against me, and it'll be more comfortable than lying down." She pointed out the patrol room building to Mr. Santiago. "See where that big red sign with the white cross is? We'll meet you there."

She climbed into the sled, and Butch helped Lizzie in after her. He tucked a blanket over Lizzie's lap. "Comfy?" he asked. Then he picked up the long handles attached to the front of the toboggan, and they were off. Sarah was right: Butch was a good driver. The ride was smooth and fast and over almost too quickly. Before she knew it, Lizzie was climbing out of the sled, guided by Butch and another patroller, who had come out of the clinic. They helped her inside and sat her down on a cot. Mr. Santiago arrived just behind them.

"We're going to need to get your jacket off," said Sarah, "so first we'll remove that sling. We'll move carefully so we don't hurt you." She threw off her own jacket and pushed up her sleeves.

When they were done with that, Sarah told Lizzie to lie down. "We'll check out your wrist a little more, and put a splint on it." Lizzie relaxed against the pillows and turned her head to look around while Sarah gently touched her wrist. The patrol clinic was nothing fancy, just a plain room with a few cots. But on the wall next to the cot she was lying on, Lizzie saw something that made her smile.

"Is that your dog?" She pointed to a calendar with a picture of a golden retriever in a bright red vest with a white cross. The dog stood in a heroic pose, with snowy mountains in the background.

Sarah glanced up at the picture as she felt Lizzie's wrist all over. "I wish. That's an avalanche dog named Jasper. He works out west with a ski patrol. We don't really have avalanches around here, but out there it's a real danger. Those dogs are trained to find someone who has been buried in snow."

"Like a search-and-rescue dog?" Lizzie asked.

"Exactly," said Sarah. "Only more specialized. I'm saving up for a golden retriever of my own, from the same breeder who raised and trained Jasper. Hopefully someday I'll be patrolling with my new best friend." She pushed back on her wheeled stool. "Good news," she said. "I don't think your wrist is broken. It's probably just a bad sprain. You might even be able to get back on your board within a day or two."

She turned to Mr. Santiago. "If the swelling and pain haven't gotten better in a few hours, you could take her to the hospital for an X-ray, but I don't think it's necessary."

Sarah wrapped a plastic bag full of snow around Lizzie's wrist, then taped on a cardboard splint that would help keep her arm still. "Keep icing it off and on until dinnertime at least," Sarah said. "I bet it will feel better by the time you're eating dessert."

After they'd thanked everybody, Lizzie and Mr. Santiago walked back to their lodge. Lizzie glanced up at the ski trails. Now that she felt good on her snowboard, she was almost sorry she had to stay off the slopes. Then she remembered Zipper, and she smiled. At least now she would be able to spend as much time as she liked with the "little troublemaker."

CHAPTER EIGHT

Mr. Santiago helped Lizzie settle herself on one of the couches near the fireplace at the lodge, with Zipper on the floor next to her. Annie brought her some pillows and a blanket, and Josef brought her hot chocolate and a plate piled high with freshly baked banana bread. Maria lent Lizzie her iPod. Dillon, who'd heard about her accident from Josef and Annie, stopped by and helped her finish off all the banana bread while Lizzie told him about her adventures. Even Zipper seemed to understand that she was hurt. He sat quietly on the floor next to the couch, pushing his nose into her good hand and snuffling softly.

Suddenly, Lizzie was exhausted. She fell asleep with her hand on Zipper's head.

When she woke up, Mrs. Santiago was perched on the couch next to her, feeling her forehead. The cool hand on her face almost made Lizzie want to burst into tears.

"Poor thing," said Mrs. Santiago. "I'm so sorry — I only heard about it when I came in for lunch."

"I'm okay," said Lizzie. "My wrist still hurts, but I don't have a fever or anything."

Mrs. Santiago smiled. "I know. It's just a habit, I guess. The first thing I always check when Maria's not feeling well." She kept her hand on Lizzie's head. "You must be missing your mom."

"My parents!" Lizzie sat up. "I haven't even called them yet."

"Shhh," said Mrs. Santiago. "We called them. They know you're hurt, and that you're going to be fine. But, Lizzie, I want to ask you something.

Do you want to go home early? Maybe you're feeling a little homesick?"

Lizzie thought for a second. She knew what being homesick felt like. She had felt it when she went to the Santiagos' cabin that time. But surprisingly, she wasn't feeling it now. Sure, she would be happy to see her mom and dad, and even her brothers. But everybody was being so nice to her. She didn't feel at all lonely or sad.

"I'm okay," Lizzie said again. "I definitely want to stay." She would feel terrible if the Santiagos cut their vacation short just for her. Anyway, even with her hurt wrist, she was still having a good time — especially since she had Zipper to keep her company.

That night after dinner, as she finished off the last bite of her brownie sundae, she realized that Sarah had been right. Her wrist did feel better! It looked less swollen, too.

"Great!" said Maria when Lizzie shared the news. "Maybe we can go snowboarding again tomorrow."

"Uh, I don't think so," said Mr. Santiago. "Lizzie should take it easy for at least another day." He turned to Lizzie. "I was hoping that you would come snowshoeing with me tomorrow. We can relax around here in the morning and then go out after lunch. I saw some interesting tracks today and I wanted to go back and check them out again. I think it might have been a bobcat!"

"Can Zipper come?" Lizzie asked, reaching down to pet the sleepy dog, who lay at her feet.

"I suppose so," he answered. "I'm sure he'd love to get out, and we did promise Dillon that we'd take good care of him. But you'd better let me hold his leash so you don't hurt your arm. I promise to hang on more tightly from now on."

In the morning, Lizzie's wrist hurt even less and looked almost normal. She felt a pang as she watched Maria and her mom head off for another day on the slopes after breakfast. She had almost been looking forward to graduating to the chairlift and some real hills. At least she had learned the basics, and she wasn't so scared anymore.

Lizzie was cuddling with Zipper near the fireplace when Annie called to her. "Lizzie, you have a visitor."

A moment later, Sarah walked into the lounge.

"Hi!" said Lizzie. "I was going to come see you and thank you later on. You were totally right about my wrist being better by dessert time last night. And look at it now!" She held up her wrist.

"Excellent," said Sarah as she knelt to pet Zipper. "I thought maybe I could take this guy out for a walk, if that would be helpful." She smiled at Lizzie. "I know Dillon's dogs have a lot of energy."

"How do you know Dillon?" Lizzie asked.

"Tilden is a small town," Sarah said. "Dillon and I went to high school together. In a town this small, everybody knows everybody else — and their business, too. But I didn't know Dillon was looking for a new home for his pup, until you said you were fostering him. That's interesting."

Lizzie dozed off while Sarah took Zipper out. When she woke, Zipper was lying by her side again and Josef was calling, "Lunchtime!"

"Ready?" asked Mr. Santiago after they'd eaten lunch. "I borrowed a pair of snowshoes for you, so we're all set."

Lizzie adjusted Zipper's harness. His eyes were bright with excitement. "I'm ready, and Zipper's ready, too," she said.

Mr. Santiago took the leash, and Zipper trotted happily along next to him with his ears up and his tail wagging eagerly.

Oh, boy! Oh, boy! Now where are we going?

They picked up the snowmobile trail right across the road from the lodge. "We'll take this for a while," said Mr. Santiago. "It's easier to walk on the packed trail. Once we get into the woods, there are some other paths we can take. They all crisscross this trail, so we can't get lost."

They clomped along in their snowshoes, with Zipper leading the way. He roved from side to side, sniffing at trees and occasionally pawing at the snow. Lizzie loved watching him prance along. He was interested in everything. She had never seen a dog who was more curious about the world.

After a while, Mr. Santiago turned off the snow-mobile trail onto a smaller trail made by other snowshoers. They followed that for a while, then crossed the snowmobile trail again and struck out in another direction. Now they were the ones making the trail. "We're really getting deep into the woods," said Mr. Santiago. "Isn't it beautiful here?"

Lizzie looked around. It *was* beautiful. They were surrounded by pine trees, some towering over their heads and some so small and snow-covered that they looked like little white gnomes. The air was crisp and clean and full of — "Snow!" Lizzie twirled around with her face to the sky. Big fat snowflakes drifted lazily through the trees, dancing on their way down. A huge flake landed on Zipper's forehead.

"That's right, they did say it might snow a bit today," said Mr. Santiago. "It'll wipe out all the animal tracks for a while, but I'm sure the skiers and boarders will be very happy about it."

They continued on until they came across the snowmobile trail again. Zipper's tail went up and he charged down the trail, pulling Mr. Santiago after him. "He must be used to running on these trails with Dillon," Mr. Santiago yelled over his shoulder as he clomped after Zipper.

It wasn't easy to keep up. Lizzie was starting to feel tired, and her wrist had begun to throb. "If I turn around and follow this trail back, it'll go straight to the lodge, right?" she asked Mr. Santiago. "I think I'm ready for a rest."

"We'll come with you," he said. He tried to turn back toward Lizzie, but Zipper pulled hard in the other direction. The rangy pup was obviously not ready to finish his walk.

Lizzie waved a hand. "I'm fine," she told him. "And I think Zipper really needs the exercise. You go ahead."

Mr. Santiago frowned. "I suppose it's all right," he said. "There's no way you can get lost if you stay on the snowmobile trail. It does go straight back to the lodge. Zipper and I will turn back in just a couple of minutes. We'll be right behind you."

Lizzie gave Zipper a good-bye scratch between the ears and headed off. "'Bye!" she called. "I bet I'll be drinking hot chocolate by the time you get there."

The snow seemed to fall faster and thicker with every step Lizzie took. The air was full of flakes now, not the big fat lazy ones but smaller, serious-looking flakes. She tried to go a little faster, but her snowshoes were not made for speed.

Soon Lizzie spotted the snowshoe trail they'd taken earlier. It went off to her right. The new snow blurred the prints, but they would still be easy to follow. She stepped onto the softer snow, happy for the shortcut. When she came back out onto the snowmobile trail, she'd be much closer to the lodge.

There was only one problem.

She could not find the snowmobile trail.

CHAPTER NINE

Where was the trail? Lizzie stared through the falling snow. She knew she must have walked far enough. She should be coming to the trail any second now. She strained her ears, hoping to hear the buzzing of a snowmobile.

There was no buzz.

In fact, it was so quiet that she could hear the tiny *tick-tick* sound of snowflakes landing on her hat. She looked up to watch the swirling, dancing flakes drift down. Normally, Lizzie would have stuck out her tongue to catch a few. Not now. Not until she knew where she was.

She walked on, plodding through the deepening

snow. Every slow step seemed more difficult than the one before. Her wrist was really starting to hurt. And worst of all, the weak sunlight that had filtered into the woods earlier was beginning to fade. How could it be getting dark already? They had left the lodge right after lunch. They couldn't have been out that long — could they?

The trees seemed to press in around her. Their snow-covered branches drooped and reached downward. Before, they had looked pretty, like something on a holiday card. Now they loomed darkly, like scary monsters you'd see in a nightmare.

"Okay, that's it," said Lizzie after she'd walked a little longer. "If I don't see the snowmobile trail in twenty — no, *ten* — more steps, I'm turning around."

Ten steps later, she was only deeper into the trees. She sighed and turned around, knowing that at least she could follow her own tracks backward and start over again, taking the longer way around. This shortcut had turned into a longcut.

Lizzie kept her eyes on the ground now, searching out her tracks. It wasn't as easy as she had thought it would be. For one thing, the snow was falling so thickly now that it was already filling in the wide, fat tracks of her snowshoes. For another, it really was getting darker every minute. She couldn't pretend that it wasn't.

She pushed branches away as she trudged through the woods. The trail was narrower than she remembered. Then she came to a stream, a trickle of cold clear water shimmering over a rocky bed. A stream? She definitely did not remember that. Could she have taken a wrong turn somewhere? Lizzie spun around and headed back in the opposite direction, trying to find the spot where she had made a mistake.

Now there were snowshoe tracks all over the place. Were they all hers? Which ones were the freshest? Lizzie felt her heart beating fast. She stopped and took a deep breath. Then she listened again, hoping for some sound that would guide her back to the lodge. She didn't hear a thing.

"Maybe *I* should make some noise," Lizzie said out loud. "Mr. Santiago!" she yelled as loudly as she could. She cupped her hands over her mouth and yelled again. "Zipper! Help! Find me!"

She yelled a few more times, then let her hands fall to her sides. Her gloves were soaking wet from the snow, and her fingers felt cold and stiff. Snow slipped from a tree branch above her and trickled down the back of her neck, making her shiver.

This was not good. Lizzie closed her eyes for a moment and tried to think. What was the smartest thing to do if you were lost? Usually, she knew, you were supposed to stay in one place so people could come find you. But it was cold out, and getting dark. If she stayed in one place, she was going to freeze.

Lizzie remembered a book her mom had once read to her, about a boy who was lost on a mountain in Maine for three days. Now she was in Maine, and she was lost.

The boy had finally found his way out of the woods, starving and exhausted and covered in mosquito bites — but his adventure had happened in summer. Even when he lost his shoes and his shirt, he could keep moving. Lizzie tried to remember how he had found his way down the mountain. He had followed streams, hadn't he? Because water flowed downhill.

Lizzie looked in the direction of the stream. Should she go back and follow it? Should she stay right where she was? Or should she try again to find her way back to the snowmobile trail? Her wrist throbbed painfully. She didn't know what to do, so instead she just yelled some more. "Mr. Santiago! Zipper! Anyone! Please help!"

Now her hands were so cold they hurt. Her feet were past hurting. They were numb, like blocks of ice, and her nose was freezing. And running. She wiped at it with a wet glove and realized that her eyes were running, too. She was crying.

She hadn't cried when she fell and hurt her wrist. She hadn't cried when the ski patrollers moved it to put the splint on. She hadn't cried when she thought about how far away from home she was, without her mom or dad. But she couldn't help it anymore. She squatted down in the middle of a small clearing in the woods, and she hugged herself, and she cried.

She didn't cry for long. Soon she wiped her nose

again on the back of her glove and stood up. She couldn't just hang around crying until it got totally dark. She had to do something, She listened again. Was anybody even looking for her? She strained to hear the sound of her name being shouted.

Instead, she heard a branch snap. Then another.

A bear? Lizzie's heart pounded in her throat. No, not a bear. Bears hibernated in winter. But something was definitely coming her way. Something big, crashing through the trees. What if it was a moose?

Then she heard the jingling of collar tags. A moment later, Zipper burst into the clearing and threw himself at her, grinning his goofy grin and whining happily.

I knew it! I knew you were here!

CHAPTER TEN

Lizzie wrapped her arms around Zipper's skinny frame. "Oh, Zipper," she said. "You found me." She was crying again, but this time they were tears of relief. Zipper's body was warm and solid. She felt safe again now that he was here. Maybe he could help her find her way back to the snowmobile trail. First, though, all she wanted was to hug him. She pulled him close and he licked the side of her face, snuffling against her ear.

Then she felt his body tense up as he pushed away from her, turning to face a row of trees. His ears perked up and his whole body seemed to tremble as he focused intently.

Something's coming!

"What is it, Zipper?" Lizzie asked. She tried to hug him again, but he wouldn't relax. He sniffed the air and lifted one front foot.

Lizzie closed her eyes for a second. Was a wild animal about to pounce on them? Zipper was only a puppy. She couldn't expect him to protect her. He would probably be as scared as she was. In fact, it was her duty to protect *him*. After all, she'd promised Dillon that she would take good care of his dog.

"Lizzie? Oh, thank goodness!" Mr. Santiago crashed through the trees and into the clearing. "Are you okay?" He came over to hug her, and Zipper jumped up on both of them.

What about me? Don't I get a hug? We're all together again. Let's celebrate!

"I'm fine," said Lizzie. "Zipper found me."

"He sure did," said Mr. Santiago. "I was trying to follow your tracks, but I got all turned around. Then Zipper seemed to hear something, and he took off running with his nose to the ground. I tried to keep up, but I kept tripping over my snow-shoes. I couldn't hold on to him."

"He must have heard me yelling," said Lizzie.

Mr. Santiago took a long, deep breath. "Lucky thing he did," he said. "Now we just have to find our way out of here."

"No problem."

Where had that voice come from? Lizzie looked behind her and saw a flash of red against the trees. It was Sarah, in her ski patroller's jacket!

Lizzie stared at her. "How did you —"

"I called ski patrol as soon as I thought you might be lost," said Mr. Santiago. He turned to Sarah. "Thanks for coming."

"My pleasure," said Sarah. "I knew just where to find you. Lots of people get turned around on these trails. But I see that someone else knew how to find you, too." She walked over and dropped to one knee to pet Zipper. "What a good boy," she said, scratching his ears. Zipper's tail wagged madly, and he snuffled at her face. Then she stood up and slung off her backpack. "Are you warm enough?" she asked Lizzie. "I have an extra hat and pair of mittens in here."

The next day, Lizzie returned Sarah's red wool mittens as they stood next to each other on the snow. "Thanks again," she said. "For everything."

Sarah grinned. "I hope Zipper had some special treats when you got back to the lodge." She reached out to scratch the tall puppy's ears, and he looked up at her adoringly. Lizzie could tell that Zipper never forgot a friend.

"He sure did." Lizzie looked down at Zipper, standing at her side in his harness. "And now he gets to see his dad in a race. How cool is that?" Dillon had called Lizzie and the Santiagos to remind them about his skijoring race. It turned out that they had a perfect viewing spot, where the snowmobile trail ran right across from the Timberline Lodge. Sarah, who had the day off from patrolling, had come to watch. Annie and Josef were there, too, to cheer their nephew on.

Maria leaned to peer down the snowmobile trail. "When will we see the first racers?" she asked.

"Any minute, I bet," said her dad.

"I think I hear something," said her mom. "Are they coming?"

Zipper obviously heard something, too. He jumped up and stared into the distance.

"There they are!" yelled Lizzie as she saw the

first racer crest the hill. He was skiing like mad behind the black dog he was harnessed to. The dog charged down the trail, churning up the snow with his big paws as his long legs took huge strides. Then Lizzie saw the dog's white chest. "That's Digger. It's Dillon! He's in first!"

Sure enough, Dillon grinned and waved at them as he approached. Another racer was not far behind, a tall woman being pulled by a long-haired Siberian husky. "Go, Dillon!" Maria yelled.

"Yay, Digger!" screamed Lizzie. "Go, go!" It was amazing how fast they were moving. Digger's long tongue flapped out of his grinning mouth, and his eyes were focused on the trail. He ran easily, as if he was doing what he was born to do.

Zipper jumped up and down, barking excitedly.

In a flash, Dillon and three other racers disappeared over the next long hill.

"If we jump in the car, we should be able to get to the finish line before they do," said Mr. Santiago. "I've got it all warmed up and ready. Please join us, Sarah."

Down the hill, banners fluttered in the breeze and a large crowd had gathered. A woman's voice came over the loudspeaker, giving updates. "They're almost here, folks!" she said. "Number eight, Dillon Goss, still in the lead! Give our local racer a big hand."

Lizzie and Maria scrambled to get into a good spot for watching the finish. Here came Dillon and Digger, with the Siberian right on their heels. "Go, go!" Lizzie yelled. "You can do it, Digger!"

With a burst of speed, Dillon passed under the finish-line banner. "Yes!" he shouted, throwing a fist into the air. He clicked out of his skis and opened his arms wide to let Digger jump up on his chest. Skier and dog spun around in a happy, dancing hug.

Everybody cheered. Everybody, Lizzie noticed, but Sarah. Sarah stood watching quietly, a sad smile on her face. "What's the matter?" Lizzie asked, tugging on Sarah's jacket sleeve.

"It's just that I can see how happy Digger is. I'm sure Zipper will be just as happy once Dillon has time to train him. These dogs are built for running."

Lizzie nodded. "But why does that make you sad?"

"Because," Sarah said, "I was kind of hoping Dillon might let me adopt Zipper. I think he'd make an awesome avalanche dog."

"Wow!" Lizzie smiled. "I think you're right. He sure does have a good nose." She could picture Zipper and Sarah together, living in a mountain-top cabin in the high western mountains.

"And a curious mind, too," said Sarah. "I can't see him giving up on a search once he got started." She reached down to hug Zipper just as a panting, red-faced Dillon came over to greet them.

"Great race!" said Lizzie, giving him a big high five.

"Thanks," said Dillon. "I never could have done it without your help. Digger and I really became a team this week, once we had the time to train on our own."

He looked down at Zipper, in Sarah's arms. "I hear you and Zipper were a pretty good team, too," he said to Sarah. "One of you found Lizzie; the other helped her find her way home. That got me thinking. I already knew that Zipper needs more attention than I can give him right now, and then Lizzie mentioned that you're saving up for an avalanche dog. Is there any chance that you —"

"YES!" said Sarah and Lizzie together, before he could even finish the question.

Everyone laughed. Maria threw her arms around Lizzie. "You did it again," she said. "It's almost like magic how you always help puppies find the perfect forever homes."

"I'll even throw in some skijoring lessons," Dillon said to Sarah. "I can teach you, and Digger can teach Zipper."

"That sounds great," said Sarah. "Um — do you think I could take Zipper up to my place right now? As long as I have the day off, I'd love to get him used to my cabin."

"Why not?" Dillon asked. "It's nice to know he'll still be in town, so I won't have to really say good-bye to him." He knelt down to hug Zipper.

Lizzie bent down to pet him, too. "I hope I'll see your picture on a calendar someday," she told the long-legged pup. She was sorry to have to say good-bye to Zipper, but she knew he would have a great life with Sarah.

She stood up and turned to Maria. "My wrist doesn't hurt at all today. Are you up for a ride on the quad, now that we're off dog duty?"

"Yes!" shouted Maria.

PUPPY TIPS

As soon as I got my puppy Zipper, I knew I had to write a book about him. He is a real character, and has a special personality — just like every dog. I tried to take a lot of notes during his early puppy days, so I could remember everything about that time, and I still write about him in my journal almost every day.

It makes me love my dog even more to write down all the special things about him: what toy he loves to play with, where he likes to sleep, what makes me laugh about him, who his doggie best friends are, what tricks he has learned. Try it! You might even end up writing a whole book about your dog, just like I did.

Dear Reader,

"Are your books real, or made up?" I get that question a lot from my readers. The answer is always complicated. My stories are made up, but there are often a lot of "real" parts to them, too.

In this book, almost everything about Zipper is "real." His Nosey Parker personality, his looks, the way his yawn sounds like a creaky gate, his happy outlook on life, the way he chews through leashes — even his father's name (Digger)! Zipper is a Eurohound, and I got him from a family who raises — and races — sled dogs. One of the boys in the family is named Dillon, and he is a skijoring champion. Last winter, Dillon and Digger gave me a skijoring lesson!

Another "real" part is about ski patrolling. I used to be a ski patroller — not at the made-up Bear Valley, but at a resort in Vermont called Bolton Valley, where I still love to ski. All the details about the toboggan ride and the splint on Lizzie's arm come from my experience as a patroller.

The characters of Josef and Annie and Sofie are based on my good friends and their dog. They don't own an inn, but Joe loves to cook and I love to go to their house for dinner. Anne is an artist who loves to draw dogs and cats. Sofie is very good at helping to wash the dishes.

ABOUT THE AUTHOR

Ellen Miles loves dogs, which is why she has a great time writing the Puppy Place books. And guess what? She loves cats, too! (In fact, her very first pet was a beautiful tortoiseshell cat named Jenny.) That's why she came up with the Kitty Corner series. Ellen lives in Vermont and loves to be outdoors every day, walking, biking, skiing, or swimming, depending on the season. She also loves to read, cook, explore her beautiful state, play with dogs, and hang out with friends and family.

Visit Ellen at www.ellenmiles.net.